LETHAL SCREAM

Dillon Fuhrman

dizzyemupublishing.com

DIZZY EMU PUBLISHING

1714 N McCadden Place, Hollywood, Los Angeles 90028

dizzyemupublishing.com

Lethal Scream
Dillon Fuhrman

First published in the United States
in 2022 by Dizzy Emu Publishing

1 3 5 7 9 10 8 6 4 2

dizzyemupublishing.com

LETHAL SCREAM

Dillon Fuhrman

<u>LETHAL SCREAM</u>

Written by

Dillon Fuhrman

Inspired by

"Scream" By Kevin Williamson

And

"Lethal Weapon" By Shane Black

Dedicated to

Richard Donner

FADE IN:

INT. WHITNEY'S HOUSE - LIVING ROOM - NIGHT

Inside a house you would see in "Good Housekeeping," Halloween decorations are adorned throughout the house. There are two occupants inside the house, WHITNEY OLSON and her boyfriend, RICK COHEN.

Whitney is a blonde-haired 17-year-old high school student while Rick is a dark brown-haired 18 year old high school student, and judging by his jaw being so squared, you might assume he is the school football team's top quarterback.

The high school golden couple watch something like Wes Craven's Scream all the while making out, but soon stop when Rick notices a statue of Freddy Krueger at the edge of the hallway, scaring him.

WHITNEY
What?

RICK
I can't believe your folks have that realistically creepy looking Freddy Krueger in the house.

WHITNEY
Tell me about it: My dad paid good money for that, and it's still in tip-top shape.

RICK
(beat)
I can't believe your dad, on his salary, would buy something that creepy, and now, we can't have sex with that thing looking at us.

WHITNEY
It's an inanimate object, Rick.

RICK
But still.
(to the TV)
Wes Craven's Scream: Hands down the best horror film of the 90s.

WHITNEY
Oh, come on.

RICK
What?

WHITNEY
I Know What You Did Last Summer is the better of the two.

RICK
Why? Because of your massive girl crush on Jennifer Love Hewitt?

WHITNEY
For your information: Sarah Michelle Gellar is the better scream queen than Jennifer Big Boobs. And better actress as well.

RICK
Yeah: Cruel Intentions.

WHITNEY
Oh, please!

RICK
What?

WHITNEY
Tell me that lesbian scene between Sarah Michelle Gellar and Selma Blair didn't pop in your head when you said that?

RICK
(stammering)
Ah...wha...we...No.

WHITNEY
You men: All you think about is girls having hot lesbo sex, and because of your perverted mind: Go cook us some fucking popcorn.

With the bowl in hand, Rick leaves the room.

INT. WHITNEY'S HOUSE - KITCHEN

Raiding the cupboards, Rick spots PopSecret. He then removes the wrapping, places the bag in the microwave, and presses the Popcorn button, activating the microwave. Unbeknownst to him, someone dressed in military garb, holding a knife, approaches Rick, silencing him.

INT. WHITNEY'S HOUSE - LIVING ROOM

Hearing the commotion, Whitney mutes the television.

WHITNEY
Rick? Rick, is everything okay in there?

Then, someone with a big bowl of popcorn exits the kitchen, switching off the lights. Then, Whitney unmutes the television. Approaching the loveseat, the shadowy figure places the popcorn down, and caresses Whitney's face and upper body.

WHITNEY (CONT'D)
(aroused)
Rick, Rick: What about Freddy?

Suddenly, the figure goes from caressing Whitney to outright strangling her. Then, Whitney turns her head and sees the person strangling her, and stabs her attacker with a pen. Escaping his grasp, Whitney rushes upstairs.

INT. WHITNEY'S HOUSE - WHITNEY'S BEDROOM

Entering her princess-like bedroom, Whitney locks the door, and snatches her phone, calling the police, but nothing is getting through. Then, the attacker starts bashing the door down. Without any options, Whitney exits through the window.

Finally inside Whitney's room, the attacker sees the window open, and rushes out the room.

EXT. WOODS

Inside the dark void that is the woods, Whitney runs like Usain Bolt, but suddenly, out of nowhere, the attacker stands in front, lifts Whitney off the ground, and stabs her in the chest.

Throwing Whitney down, the attacker slices her to death with the skill of a butcher.

DISSOLVE TO:

INT. MERCER HOUSE - MOLLY'S ROOM - DAY

Getting ready for work, MOLLY MERCER, late 50s, red-haired, and has Ava Gardner-like beauty, dresses herself. Then, her kids: OLIVIA, MAX, and NATALIE surprise their mother.

Olivia is the eldest; she is 16-years-old. Max is the middle child; he is eight-years-old. Natalie is the youngest; she is six-years-old.

KIDS
Surprise!

MOLLY
(startled)
Whoa: You scared me.

NATALIE
Sorry, Mommy: We just wanted to surprise you since you got that promotion.

MAX
We made this cake in honor of it.

MOLLY
Oh, guys: Thank you. It means a lot.
(hugging her kids)
You three don't know how special you made this day.

OLIVIA
Well, we wanted to make sure that it was.

MOLLY
And you three succeeded: Listen, why don't you go downstairs, finish your breakfast, and I'll take you to school.

NATALIE
Aren't you worried about being late?

MOLLY
(picking up her badge)
I'm the new Police Detective, sweetheart: I'm not worried about being late. Besides, it's a 24/7 job.

NATALIE
Cool.
(to Max)
Race you down the stairs.

Once Max and Natalie leave, Olivia stays.

MOLLY
Something wrong, sweetheart?

OLIVIA
Nothing, it's just...I hope this promotion means you'll still be able to spend time with Max, Natalie, and I.

MOLLY
Of course, why wouldn't it?

OLIVIA
You said it was a 24/7 job.

MOLLY
What I meant by that is that I'm on-call 24/7, but if any one of you have an event, I would rather focus on that as opposed to my job.
(a long beat)
You three mean the world to me, and I'm always going to be there for you.

OLIVIA
Promise?

MOLLY
I promise.

Mother and daughter hug.

MOLLY (CONT'D)
Get ready for school.

OLIVIA
Yes, ma'am.
(beat)
Oh, by the way, before you came home, some guy named Calvin called the house.

MOLLY
Calvin? Calvin? His last name wouldn't be Olson would it?

OLIVIA
I think so: Why do you ask?

MOLLY
Oh, he used to be a old friend of mine.

OLIVIA
Are you two still friends?

MOLLY
I don't know: I haven't spoken to him in twenty years.

OLIVIA
That long, huh?

MOLLY
You would be surprised: Now, go get ready for school, and tell those little munchkins to get ready as well.

OLIVIA
Yes, Mom.

As Olivia leaves the room, Molly opens her top dresser drawer, and finds a photo of herself and a man that doesn't look like her husband; they are wearing wedding attire. A faint smile comes across Molly's face.

I/E. JACK'S TRAILER

Inside a somewhat messy trailer, JACK COLT, late-30s, Black, and hungover, falls off the couch, and heads to the kitchen, snagging a bottle of Jack Daniel's. He wears dogtags around his neck. A beat.

Opening the bottle, Jack drinks it, and then gives kibble and fresh water to his pug, Porsha. She is the cutest little pug in the whole world, and the only thing Jack loves in his messy life.

JACK
Here you go, sweetie.

Sitting back down on the couch, Jack turns on the television, and flips through channels. He stops when reruns of the 1960s Batman show appears. Porsha, after she finished eating, jumps on the couch and cuddles with her daddy.

Spotting his wedding ring, a tearful Jack puts it on, and pets his pug.

EXT. WOODS - DAY - LATER

After dropping her children of at school, Molly heads to a crime scene, a nice way to start off her first day as a detective. Exiting her 2014 Kia Soul, Molly is approached by a PATROLMAN.

PATROLMAN
Detective Mercer, congratulations on your promotion, ma'am.

MOLLY
Thank you: What's the situation?

PATROLMAN
Young girl and her boyfriend were found butchered and hung up on a tree like puppets. A jogger found them this morning.

When they approach the crime scene, Molly sees Whitney and Rick's dead bodies, with their guts spilled out and wide open for everyone to see, still hanging on the tree. Molly becomes disgusted.

MOLLY
Cut them down.

PATROLMAN
Yes, ma'am.
(to his associate)
McGinty, cut them down.

MOLLY
Did you I.D. the victims?

PATROLMAN
We did: The boyfriend's name is Rick Cohen, and the girlfriend's name is Whitney Olson.

MOLLY
Say that again?

PATROLMAN
The boyfriend's name is Rick Co--

MOLLY
No, no: The girlfriend's name: Did you say her last name is Olson?

PATROLMAN
That's correct.

MOLLY
Does her last name have an "E?"

PATROLMAN
No, it has an "O." Do you know her, ma'am?

MOLLY
I knew her father.

PATROLMAN
Do you want me to call the parents?

MOLLY
No: I'll do it.

Snagging her cellphone, Molly calls Olivia.

OLIVIA (O.S.)
(answering)
Hello?

MOLLY
Hey, sweetie: Are you busy?

OLIVIA (O.S.)
No, why?

MOLLY
Do you know Calvin's number by any chance?

EXT. LOS ANGELES PUMPKIN PATCH

On the other side of town, Jack observes an array of firearms with a bunch of drug dealers: MIGUEL, JUAN, HAROLD, and KENT.

MIGUEL
What do you think: You like the shipment?

JACK
I like it. I'll take a couple of freights.

HAROLD
Yo, my man: The deal was for one freight.

JACK
Can a guy like me change his mind? I mean, it's a free country last time I checked, right?

KENT
Yes, but when you do business with us, you honor the arrangement we set. Comprendo, fucker?

MIGUEL
Take it easy, gents: If the man wants two freights, we'll give him two freights.

JACK
See that, guys: You should listen to the boss more often. How much?

MIGUEL
Three-hundred.

Snatching his wallet, Jack lays fifteen 20 dollar bills. The dealers are perplexed.

JUAN
What the fuck is this?

JACK
Hey, shut up: You'll mess up my count. Forty. No, no. Sixty.

Fed up, Miguel stabs the pumpkin next to Jack.

MIGUEL
What are you doing?

JACK
You said three-hundred, and I'm doing my count.

MIGUEL
Three-hundred thousand.

JACK
Three-hundred thousand? Oh boy, I don't have that kind of money on me, sorry.

Angered, the dealers create a one-sided Mexican standoff.

JACK (CONT'D)
I'll tell you what: Why don't I get my contact in Constantinople so we can sort this mess out.

HAROLD
Hey moron, Constantinople doesn't exist anymore.

JACK
Oh, well: That's too bad because...you're under arrest.

Tossing his badge on the ground, Jack grabs his pistol, and a swarm of SWAT units converge in the pumpkin patch which soon becomes a wild west shootout. The attending patrons duck for cover or becomes embroiled in the crossfire.

As Harold, Kent, and Juan drew first blood, Jack shoots Harold and Kent dead, and wounds Juan. Suddenly, out of the shadows, Miguel holds a young girl at gunpoint when the SWAT team circles around the hostage situation.

MIGUEL
Drop the weapon, asshole!

JACK
(PTSD triggered)
Let the girl go.

MIGUEL
You drop the weapon and I'll let the girl go.

Thinking of the young hostage's well-being, Jack lowers his weapon.

JACK
(to little girl)
It's okay, honey. Everything will be all right.

MIGUEL
You cops: You always fall for everything.

In cold blood, Miguel blows the little girl's head off, setting off Jack's trauma, and rage consumes him. Lunging toward the murderous drug dealer, Jack brutally beats Miguel to a pulp with his bare hands, causing the fellow boys in blue to fear him.

VOICE
THAT'S ENOUGH!

Suddenly, Jack spots his boss, Captain THERESA GRANT. The sight of his boss causes Jack to release a fully incapacitated Miguel and cool off. The SWAT team arrest Miguel and Juan. A furious Grant approaches Jack. Shee is a no-nonsense woman pushing 70-years-old.

GRANT
(furious)
My office: Today.

JACK
Yes, ma'am.

After that, Jack has tears flowing down.

INT. CAPTAIN'S OFFICE - DAY - LATER

SLAMMMING on her DESK, Grant stares at Jack.

GRANT
Why? Why did you turn a simple drug bust into a goddamn shootout? People will now have to mourn their loved ones who were used as human shields.

JACK
(remorseful)
I know.

GRANT
Not only that, you could've gotten your colleagues killed.

JACK
But they weren't, Captain. Besides, we got the head honcho of the cartel, didn't we?

GRANT
Yes, but still: Your reckless disregard for police procedures caused some people to die today, and now the blood is on your hands.
(a long beat)
So, instead of suspending you, you are to be reassigned to homicide, and demoted back to Detective First Class.

JACK
But, that's not fair.

GRANT
I have no choice, Jack: It is either that or a suspension, or worse: Firing you.
(beat)
Look, I know things have been pretty difficult in your life, with Adrienne--

JACK
Why don't you shut the fuck up about my personal life: Adrienne is dead, and I have come to terms with it, thanks to this job.

GRANT
Do you know what today it is, Jack?

JACK
October 6th, why?

GRANT
Today is the day Adrienne died. Not only that, this entire month brings you nothing but pain.
(a long beat)
Take the demotion and the reassignment, not just for the department's sake, but for yours as well.

JACK
You trust me working in homicide alone?

GRANT
You'll be working with Molly Mercer.

JACK
I'll do it, but I'm not working with a partner.

GRANT
I've known Molly for a long time, and she's the best cop I know, so take it or leave, Jack.

JACK
(relenting)
I'll report to Homicide tomorrow.

INT. JACK'S TRAILER - NIGHT

While watching It's The Great Pumpkin, Charlie Brown, Jack observes his gun. There is one bullet in the chamber; he loads it and turns the safety off. Jack has the gun pressed against his chest, and then underneath his chin.

Feeling comfortable with where the gun is, a misty-eyed Jack struggles with the trigger, but just as he's about to kill himself, Jack lowers his weapon, turns the safety back on, and lets the floodgates out. Jack notices his and Adrienne's scrapbook.

EXT. GRAVEYARD - NIGHT

Coasting the graveyard's walkway, scrapbook and Jack Daniels in hand, Jack spots a gravestone. It reads: "ADRIENNE LEIGH COLT. 1988-2012. 'Halloween is not only about putting on a costume, but it's about finding the imagination and costume within ourselves.' Elvis Duran." A beat.

Placing the bottle on top of the gravestone, Jack opens the scrapbook and locates a photo of a visibly pregnant Adrienne and a once happy Jack designing their unborn child's room. He places the photo in front of the gravestone.

JACK
(crying)
I miss you. I miss you so much:
I'll see you soon, my love.

Then, Jack sits near the gravestone and reaches for the bottle. He takes a really big swig and observes the nighttime sky.

INT. POLICE STATION

A bunch of police officers fix up some Halloween costumes and candy, pretending to be trick-or-treating to their colleagues' offices. Meanwhile, Molly and her colleague, police psychologist LYNN MATTHEWS, 40s, converse.

MOLLY
I don't believe this shit: Grant's
setting me up with a partner.

LYNN
He ain't no rookie: This guy's the
real article.

MOLLY
What do you know about him?

LYNN
Former Special Forces sniper,
honorably discharged. Joined the
police department soon after.
(MORE)

LYNN (CONT'D)
Married his childhood sweetheart the same year, but sadly she died in a robbery gone wrong. He hasn't been the same since.

MOLLY
What do you think? Should he be reassigned to homicide?

LYNN
Personally, no: I think he needs help. He's just one bad day away from snapping and going off on everyone around him.

MOLLY
Don't give me that loose cannon bullshit: That would work in the Lethal Weapon movies, but this is real life.

LYNN
Molly, the guy is dangerous, but he is hurting inside, and I think he needs real help before he inflicts his pain onto others.

MOLLY
All right, enough about him: Did you get the photos I sent you?

LYNN
I did. Very gruesome, in my honest opinion.

MOLLY
Aside from that, what I am I dealing with?

LYNN
Judging by the way the victims were hanged, it looks like someone took their love of horror movies too far.

MOLLY
(a long beat)
That's it? Horror films? This is not the L.A. Chainsaw Massacre, Lynn!

LYNN
Look, I'm a psychologist for the LAPD, not a forensic psychologist, and this is the most plausible explanation I can give.

Just in the middle of their conversation, Molly spots Jack, reaching inside his pocket.

MOLLY
Down, everybody down.

This catches Jack and everyone off guard, and as Molly charges at Jack, she trips on a surge protector cord. She and Jack lock eyes as the latter looms over the former. Soon, Lynn also hovers over Molly. The item Jack whips out is his case of Tic-Tacs.

LYNN
Molly, meet Jack Colt: Your new partner.

Shock fills Molly's eyes as Jack lets out a faint smile.

MOLLY
God help us all.

EXT. POLICE STATION - PARKING LOT - DAY - LATER

After that embarrassing moment earlier, Molly and Jack head to the former's Kia Soul.

MOLLY
Look, I'm sorry about what happened earlier: I thought you were gonna shoot the place up.

JACK
Why? Is it because I'm black?

MOLLY
No: I didn't say that.

JACK
Relax: I'm just fucking with you.

MOLLY
(a long beat)
So, I heard that you were in the Special Forces: What war did you serve?

JACK
Operation Iraqi Freedom.

MOLLY
Nice. I used to be in the military myself.

JACK
Oh yeah: What branch and war?

MOLLY
Air Force, Vietnam.

JACK
I wasn't aware females were enlisted in Vietnam.

MOLLY
Yeah, well: I was one of the ten percent that was on the battlegrounds.

JACK
Look, let's get past the bullshit: I don't like this any more than you do, but unfortunately, I had no choice because our captain wanted to suspend me, fire me, or partner with you. Fortunately, I like this job too much, so I chose option C.

MOLLY
Yeah, well: Join the club. I'm pissed at our captain also because of this. Personally, I would love to have a partner, just someone not like you.

JACK
Because I'm black?

MOLLY
Because I heard you're a loose cannon, and I'm not going to let you jeopardize my safety.

JACK
Don't worry, I'll try not to, but I still don't like this partnership.

MOLLY
Neither do I: I feel like God is giving me the "fuck you" every time something good in my life happens.

JACK
If it makes you happy, I'm an atheist.

MOLLY
Very.

The feuding partners enter the Kia Soul.

INT. ABANDONED HIGH SCHOOL - DAY - LATER

A group of government AGENTS enters an abandoned high school. They spot MISTER LOOMIS and his men front and center of the gymnasium. Loomis is a dark-haired man in his 30s, and fiercely loyal to the colonel.

AGENT #1
What the hell is this? I thought we would be meeting at an abandoned military base, not some fucking high school.

LOOMIS
Plan's changed, and if you want to speak to colonel, you'll have to speak to me first.

AGENT #1
Who the fuck are you?

LOOMIS
Rule number one: No names. But if insist, you can call me Mister Loomis. Rule number two: No swearing in front of the colonel, or me.

AGENT #1
Why? What happens?

LOOMIS
Last time someone in your position did that: They had their dick and balls cut off and sent to Washington as message.

AGENT #1
You both are sick fucks, Loomis.

LOOMIS
Swear one more time, your dick and balls are history.

Entering the lunchroom, the agents, led by Loomis, approach the colonel himself: ALAN LANCASTER. Lancaster is in his late fifties, ruthless, humorless, and has an asshole complex.

LOOMIS (CONT'D)
(approaching his superior)
Sir, they're here.

LANCASTER
Gentlemen, welcome.

AGENT #1
Colonel Lancaster, pleasure to meet you, sir. Obviously, Washington sent us here to ensure that their funds are being well spent on the program.

LANCASTER
Oh, it is: Don't you worry. Do you have a knife?

AGENT #1
A what?

LANCASTER
A knife? Steak knife, butcher knife, any kind of knife would do?

Snagging a utility knife from his jacket pocket, the lead agent hands it to Lancaster, who then hands it to Loomis. Unbuttoning his sleeve, Loomis cuts through the skin of his arm.

AGENT #1
What the hell is he doing?

LANCASTER
Showcasing you how the project is going. As you can see, Mister Loomis is our first test subject.

LOOMIS
But unlike our current test subjects, I happen to be in control of my brain. There is no way our scientists are going Manchurian Candidate on me.

AGENT #1
(unnerved)
You guys are fucking sick.

LANCASTER
What did you say, son?

AGENT #1
You guys are sick.

LANCASTER
No, no: What you said in between "are" and "sick," what did you say?

AGENT #1
(frightened)
It just slipped out, sir: Loomis warned me, and I didn't know what he was going to do.

LANCASTER
(to his men)
Grab him.

AGENT #1
Oh please, Colonel: It was a Freudian slip.

LANCASTER
Take him back with the subjects: Let him see what we got cooking.

Dragging the already frightened lead agent into the kitchen, he stumbles upon the test subjects, resting on reclined chairs, observing something high above the ceiling, television monitors. Then, the monitors turn off, and the test subjects surround the screaming agent and devour him.

Observing the massacre outside the plexiglass, Lancaster and Loomis look proud while the other government agents look shocked.

LANCASTER (CONT'D)
Let that be a lesson for the rest of you: If anyone crosses me or my men, they get this. Now, when you go back to Washington, show them this.

Suddenly, the lead agent's severed arm crashes on the glass. Removing the glass, Lancaster snatches the arm and presents it to the agents.

LANCASTER (CONT'D)
And let Washington know that we'll have our subjects ready for combat next month. Now go.

With the severed arm of their boss in tow, the remaining agents leave the high school.

LOOMIS
Let's hope they don't shut us down.

LANCASTER
They won't: The arm is a message for the bureaucratic pricks in Washington in case they do.
(beat)
Come on: We got work to do.

INT. VA CLINIC - DAY - LATER

Entering the local VA clinic, Molly and Jack spot CALVIN OLSON. He is Whitney's surviving father and is in his late 50s. Calvin is Molly's first husband in the picture, but like Molly, he's older. Recognizing Molly, Calvin approaches her.

CALVIN
God, Molly: You haven't aged a day.

MOLLY
I can say the same about you.

CALVIN
Well, no smoking and no fast food can do wonders.

MOLLY
Can we talk?

CALVIN
Yeah.

With Jack sitting outside, Molly and Calvin head inside the latter's office.

MOLLY
I appreciate you answering my call, and I am sorry it was under tragic circumstances.

CALVIN
I still appreciate that you did. If the news about Whitney came from someone else, it would've been devastating.

MOLLY
What about your wife: Does she know?

CALVIN
Yeah. I told her right away. She's been taking it not too well, but at least we have three other kids to hold us together.

MOLLY
Calvin, do you know why Whitney was killed?

CALVIN
Oh for God's sakes, Molly.

MOLLY
I'm just asking as an officer of the law, and as a friend: I want to help bring down the person responsible for Whitney's murder.

CALVIN
To be honest: I don't know why Whitney was murdered. She's been a very good person to her classmates, her teachers, and the community at large.

MOLLY
One more question: Why did you try to call me?

CALVIN
What do you mean?

MOLLY
My daughter said you tried to call my house. Why?

CALVIN
I wanted to catch up: I haven't spoken to you since our divorce. I wanted to make up to you, and apologize for how things ended between us.

Unbeknownst to the former spouses, Jack overhears.

CALVIN (CONT'D)
In return, I want you to do a favor.

MOLLY
What?

CALVIN
When you find the person responsible, kill him.

MOLLY
Calvin, I'm a cop: I have a legal responsibility.

CALVIN
I don't care if you're a goddamn cop: When you find him, kill him. Just kill him.

Breaking down into tears, Calvin leans into Molly's shoulder. She then places Calvin in her seat.

MOLLY
Send Clarissa my condolences.

CALVIN
(beat)
Molly, please.

MOLLY
I'll see you around.

Once Molly and Jack leave the clinic, a grief-stricken Calvin bows his head.

I/E. KIA SOUL - DAY - LATER

Heading to the high school Whitney attended, silence fills the car.

JACK
So, you two were married before?

MOLLY
What?

JACK
The victim's father: You and he were former spouses?

MOLLY
I was married, but that was a long time ago.

JACK
Boy, talk about a small world.
(beat)
Did you have any children together?

MOLLY
No. Calvin and I, before we even married, never felt the desire to have children. So, I had my tubes tied and my eggs frozen in storage.

JACK
I bet that made the sex life easier.

MOLLY
It did, and honestly, when I was with him, we felt lucky that I didn't get pregnant.

JACK
So, what happened?

MOLLY
Fifteen years into our marriage, my sister gave birth to her first child, and when I gazed into my niece's eyes, I fell in love with the idea of being a mother. I told Calvin, and he initially was apprehensive about it, but warmed up to the idea, so the doctors fixed my tubes and reinserted my eggs into my body. It took us four years to make a baby, and one day, I was pregnant.

JACK
I bet that made you and Calvin happy.

MOLLY
It did, and made our exercise room into the baby's room. Not only that, we found out it was a boy.
(pulling the car over)
Here.

Grabbing a photo of a very pregnant Molly and Calvin at a baby shower, revealing their baby's gender.

MOLLY (CONT'D)
On the ninth month, my water broke, but as I was delivering Samuel.

JACK
You had the name picked out?

MOLLY
We did, but as I was giving birth to Samuel, we found out that he had a weak heart and once he was born, he would only have a few hours to live. So, once Samuel was born, Calvin and I spent time with Samuel in his first and last remaining days on Earth. Once Samuel died, Calvin and I haven't been the same since.

JACK
And that's why you divorced Calvin because he reminded you of the loss of your son.

MOLLY
That and Calvin screamed at me for undoing a good thing we had of not having children.

JACK
Do you think he's right?

MOLLY
Back then, yes: But, that was when we were grieving for Samuel, but now: I don't think he's right, and I am glad I have three wonderful children with someone I adored.

JACK
Adored?

MOLLY
After I divorced Calvin, I met my husband at a bar, and I fell for him instantly: He was charming, funny, and all-around nice guy, but unlike Samuel's birth, our children's birth went smoothly.

JACK
What happened to your husband?

MOLLY
There was a storm, and he was on his way home from work to be with us, but the storm was so violent, a tree branch broke off, went through the windshield, and stabbed him in the heart, causing his car to go off road.

JACK
(a long beat)
I'm sorry, Molly. I know this is my first day being your partner and I don't know you very well, but hearing your story, I get why you're angry at God.

MOLLY
Thank you.
(beat)
We're here.

INT. HIGH SCHOOL - DAY

The two mismatched detectives interrogate Whitney's friends, AMELIA KENSINGTON, MARK KINKADE, and BROOKE DARRINGER. They are the same age as Whitney. There is an uncomfortable silence between the interrogators and the interrogatees.

JACK
It seems you three haven't answered our questions.

AMELIA
(playing with her hair)
I'm sorry, what was the question?

JACK
You're best friend was murdered two nights ago, and we are wondering why she died.

MOLLY
We were hoping you can give us some insight on anyone who might have a grudge against Whitney.

MARK
(playing with his phone)
Maybe Amy Myers.

MOLLY
Amy Myers?

BROOKE
(chewing gum obnoxiously)
She's the school slut.

JACK
Why would you say that?

BROOKE
She practically gives teachers, the entire football team, and people who do her homework a blowjob.

MOLLY
And do you know this for a fact?

MARK
Um, yeah: She invited me to her house a while back to do her homework. She tried pulling my pants down to give me a blowjob, but I stopped her and told her that I'm gay.

JACK
Have you reported this to the school?

MARK
No, I just find it funny actually.

JACK
Sexual assault is no laughing matter, son. In fact...

INT. HIGH SCHOOL - CLASSROOM

In the middle of an exam, AMY MYERS secretly using a cheating mechanism when all of a sudden, Jack bursts in.

JACK
Amy Myers?

AMY
Yeah.

JACK
(approaching Amy)
You're under arrest. You have the right to remain silent. Anything you say will be used against you in the court--

MOLLY
Jack, what are you doing?

JACK
I'm arresting her before she sexually assaults any more of her peers.

AMY
What are you talking about? I never sexually assaulted anyone.

JACK
Tell that to Mark Kinkade. The poor guy you tried to give a blowjob to without his consent.
(beat)
Anything you say will be used in the court of law. You have the right to an attorney, we'll provide one for you. Do you understand your rights? DO YOU UNDERSTAND YOUR RIGHTS?

AMY
(teary-eyed)
Yes.

Once he has Amy in handcuffs, Jack escorts her out of the building. Molly follows suit.

EXT. HIGH SCHOOL

Once outside, Jack puts Amy in the back of the Kia Soul.

MOLLY
Jack, this is crazy: You can't go around and arrest everyone on the fly.

JACK
Oh, you think sexual assault is okay?

MOLLY
No, I do not: I think we should've asked how long ago that happened because there are statute of limitations.

JACK
(noticing a jumper)
Oh my God!

Molly turns around and sees BEN SWOPE, leading a "HALLOWEEN SUCKS" march. He is a high school science teacher in his mid-30s, and wears an "I HATE HALLOWEEN" T-Shirt.

JACK (CONT'D)
What the hell is this?

MOLLY
People protesting the Halloween holiday.

JACK
Get SWAT down here. I have a bad feeling about this.

Jack then bolts toward the protesters.

MOLLY
Jack, Jack: Ah, shit!

JACK
(to protesters)
Excuse me, excuse me: Jack Colt, LAPD. Mind telling me what this protest is all about!

BEN
We have a right to march on these streets. We have a right to protest the holiday that is Halloween.

JACK
I can see that. Might I ask why you and your followers are performing this silly protest?

BEN
Kids today don't understand the significance of Halloween. They think it's all about sexy get-ups, candy bars, and haunted houses.

JACK
(beat)
Look, I get it: If you think you hate Halloween, consider me the Ebenezer Scrooge of Halloween.

BEN
You don't like Halloween?

JACK
For personal reasons, yeah.

In the distance, Molly uncuffs and releases Amy and observes the conversation between Jack and Ben.

BEN
Oh jeez, man: I'm sorry.

JACK
Thanks.

BEN
If you want, man, you are more than welcome to join our protest so you, me, and my band of anti-Halloween people can honor Adrienne.

JACK
As much as I want to, Mister...

BEN
Swope. Ben Swope.

JACK
Swope, it would be tone-deaf to disrespect my wife and her favorite holiday. That and I'm also a cop, so I will have to respectfully decline. Have a nice day, sir.

Thinking he defused the situation through non-violent means, Jack turns the other way.

BEN
Fuck you, man.

JACK
Yeah, I get that a lot.

BEN
And fuck your wife.

JACK
(losing his patience)
What did you just say?

BEN
Adrienne doesn't deserve a man like you. In fact, you are the one that got her killed.

Pissed off, Jack jumps at Ben, and beats the shit out of him. Observing this, Molly rushes to Jack's aid.

MOLLY
Goddamnit!

As Jack takes on the anti-Halloween protesters, he whips out his gun and fires it in the air, Then, the fearful protestors flee. Suddenly, the SWAT team arrives and rounds up the protesters. Soon after, a furious Molly approaches Jack.

MOLLY (CONT'D)
I'd like to speak to you.

JACK
What?

MOLLY
Come here.

With Jack following Molly, she leads him underneath the stairs.

MOLLY (CONT'D)
Okay: No more bullshit. Is this some act or is this who you really are?

JACK
What do you mean? He said he was glad my wife's dead.

MOLLY
Shut up: Just shut up. Are you that suicidal that you would be willing do die on the job?

JACK
I got the job done.

MOLLY
Just answer the fucking question, Jack?

JACK
What do you want from me, Molly? Do you want to know that every time I clock out and go home, I get lonely? Yes. Every single day, I go home and contemplate suicide, but you know the funny thing is: I love this job too much to not go through with it, and at least I come home to a pet who I adore.

MOLLY
Okay, Mister Suicidal: Take my gun and pull the trigger. Go on, use it. Use it, goddamnit!

JACK
(gun to head)
Don't push me, Molly.

MOLLY
Go on, do it: I dare you. Or better yet, put it under the chin. That way the bullet will go through your brain.

JACK
Yeah, and all the brain matter will decorate the fucking school. Or, how about the gut, the bullet will be so deep in my body, doctors will have a tough time finding it.

MOLLY
Yeah.

JACK
Yeah. Let's do it, baby.

With the safety off, Jack slowly presses the trigger as Molly realizes that his suicidal diatribe is not an act at all, thus turning her anger into fear. Then, just in the nick of time, Molly puts her finger on the trigger, thus preventing Jack's attempted suicide.

MOLLY
This is not some kind of act for attention: You really are suicidal.

JACK
I need coffee. I'll go wait in the car.

Once Jack leaves, Molly is consumed with guilt; she could have gotten someone killed on her watch, especially her partner.

MOLLY
(to herself)
Oh God. Oh God.

EXT. COFFEE SHOP - DAY - LATER

Waiting outside for Jack, Molly is on the phone with Lynn.

LYNN (O.S.)
I don't know: I told Grant that he should seek psychiatric help, but she refused, still thinking that Colt's whole death wish act is all a ploy to seek psycho pension.

MOLLY
But you beg to differ?

LYNN (O.S.)
Exactly.

MOLLY
And you think I should watch my back?

LYNN (O.S.)
Most definitely because if he becomes unglued, don't stand in his way.

MOLLY
Thank you, Lynn: Thank you for easing my mind about Colt.
(hanging up)
God help us all.

JACK
(carrying coffee cups)
I got us some coffee.

MOLLY
I don't need coffee right now. Get in the car.

Once the mismatched partners enter the Kia Soul, Molly drives off.

I/E. KIA SOUL

As Jack drinks his coffee, Molly becomes flustered.

MOLLY
(to herself)
Forty years on the force, and three promotions away from making captain, I get this.

JACK
You all right, Molly?

MOLLY
Why did she make you my partner? Huh? What was the point of having a nutcase for a partner?

JACK
Um, Molly: You should keep your eyes on the road.

MOLLY
Don't tell me how to drive, and why am I listening to you? I get the biggest promotion of my career and this is the thanks I get from God.

After calming down, Molly focuses on the road.

JACK
I didn't know that.

MOLLY
Know what?

JACK
I didn't know you were promoted. Congratulations.

MOLLY
Thanks. You're a day late, but thanks.

JACK
Well, if we get through this case, I can buy you a gift. You know, to congratulate you on your promotion.

MOLLY
Thanks: I'll take you up on your offer.

The partners share a smile.

JACK
Are you gonna tell me where we're going?

MOLLY
I've been thinking about Amy Myers.

JACK
The girl you let go?

MOLLY
You were right, and I was wrong: I talked to Whitney's male friend, and found out that it was a week ago when the incident occurred.

JACK
What about statute of limitations?

MOLLY
The statute of limitations varies, but generally, it's for more than one year. However, I think you arresting Miss Myers was the right call.

JACK
Thank you. For saying that. I can imagine how difficult it was for you to admit that.

MOLLY
You have no idea.

Once they approach the Myers residence, they notice the front door being unopened.

JACK
What?

MOLLY
The front door. It's open.

JACK
So?

MOLLY
There isn't any alarms going off right now.

Realizing the danger the Myers family is in, Molly and Jack exit the vehicle.

EXT. THE MYERS RESIDENCE

As Molly and Jack search the left and right side of the house, Molly sees blood splattered on the kitchen window, and then she reaches the pool area. Once there, she spots the murderer, hogtying Amy and her family's corpses.

The Myers Family are hung the same way as Whitney and Rick's corpses the day before today.

MOLLY
(aiming her gun)
Police, hands up.

The mute killer throws a knife at Molly, but fortunately, she dodges it. As the killer runs away, Jack jumps on and beats the shit out him, but stops. Once the killer is unconscious, Molly approaches Jack and their perp.

MOLLY (CONT'D)
See, that's how you arrest someone.

The killer awakens and holds Molly at knifepoint, with Jack pulling his gun out.

JACK
Put the knife down. Put down the fucking knife, man.

The mute murderer slightly knicks Molly's throat, but she punches his gut, preventing him from fully slashing her throat. Once Molly is out of the way, Jack shoots the killer point blank, immediately killing him.

With the SIRENS BLARING toward the NEIGHBORHOOD, Molly checks the murderer's pulse; he is dead. Beat.

MOLLY
Have you met anyone who hasn't met the angel of death through you?

JACK
You're still breathing.

Molly and Jack leave the crime scene.

INT. THE MYERS RESIDENCE - NIGHT

With the CSI team, patrolmen, and ambulance workers clearing out, only Jack and Molly remain.

JACK
What a mess.

MOLLY
Tell me about it: That's the same M.O. as the one who murdered Whitney and her boyfriend.

JACK
Do you think justice is served?

MOLLY
If you hadn't killed him, yes. But, I understand your reason: He was going to kill us, and what you did was self-defense. Thank you, Jack.

JACK
You're welcome.

MOLLY
I'm sorry as well.

JACK
For what?

MOLLY
About what happened at the school today. Hell, the whole day in fact. I treated you like a bitch.

JACK
You don't have to apologize, Molly.

MOLLY
I do: When I first saw you, I thought you like this Martin Riggs type guy: A cop living on the edge.

JACK
(laughs)
There's is some truth to that, but this is real life. There's more to me than meets the eye.

MOLLY
Go on.

JACK
You know, in Lethal Weapon, Mel Gibson's character has a dog that looks like Lassie, I have a pug.

MOLLY
A pug?

JACK
Pugs are way cuter, in my honest opinion.

MOLLY
Agreed. Listen, my shift ended a few minutes ago, and I was wondering if you weren't doing anything, would you like to have dinner with my family tonight?

JACK
Tonight, at your place?

MOLLY
Why not?

JACK
I'm down. Sure, I haven't had anything to eat today, so I'm game.

MOLLY
All right.

Jack and Molly head out to the Kia Soul.

INT. MORGUE - NIGHT - LATER

The body of the attacker lies on a metallic bed with the covers draping over the body. Disguised as a pathologist, Loomis enters the morgue and retrieves something in the murderers' head: a computer chip. Beat.

Once Loomis got what he came for, he cleans up his mess, packs up and leaves, but a naïve NIGHT GUARD in her early 30s notices him.

GUARD
Excuse me, sir? Visiting hours are over.

LOOMIS
It's okay, miss: I'm Dewey Weathers, pathologist for the LAPD, and I'm here doing an additional investigation regarding our mystery guest.

GUARD
I see. Did you happen to find anything?

LOOMIS
No. Unfortunately, I couldn't find anything. I'll just have to write it in my report when I get back to the office.

GUARD
Okay. Well, at least you cleaned up after yourself so, thank you for that.

LOOMIS
Sure. You have a good night.

GUARD
You too.

Once Loomis leaves, the guard observes the room, and notices fresh blood dripping down the door. The guard approaches the door, opens it and sees Loomis' handiwork. Out of nowhere, Loomis silences her.

INT. MOLLY'S HOUSE

Dinner is served, and Molly, her kids, and her guest Jack dig in.

MOLLY
Mmm, tasty.

OLIVIA
So, Mister Colt: How do you know my mom?

MOLLY
Olivia, not at the dinner table.

JACK
No, no: It's fine. Your mother and I are colleagues. Nothing more, nothing less.

NATALIE
Are you and Mommy dating?

MAX
Yeah: Our dad's dead, and she sure could have a night out with a guy.

MOLLY
Kids, kids.

JACK
Molly, it's fine. Really, it is.
(to Molly's kids)
Your mother and I are not dating. We are just partners at the police station. Nothing more, nothing less.

MOLLY
(beat)
Besides, I have a date this weekend. Just not with Jack.

JACK
I have plans this weekend too.

MAX
What kind of plans?

JACK
Fishing. I plan on going up the coast of Northern California and catch some fish.

MAX
Oh, cool: I caught five different fish.

JACK
Oh, really? What kind?

MAX
Um, I'm not really sure: Dad usually releases them once we catch the fish.

JACK
Nothing wrong with a little catch and release. I bet you and your dad had fun catching fish?

MAX
We did. He was the greatest.

JACK
I'll tell you what: If your mom and I are still friends and colleagues, I'll take you fishing one day.

MAX
Promise?

JACK
I promise.

Once Max and Jack pinky-promise each other, the latter and Molly share a smile.

I/E. MOLLY'S HOUSE - GARAGE - NIGHT - LATER

Perusing through Molly's achievements as a Air Force airwoman in Vietnam, she and Jack find her Purple Heart.

JACK
Wow: You really did serve in the Air Force during Vietnam.

MOLLY
(beat)
Yeah, and I should've received the Medal of Honor, but I got that handed to me as compensation for having a gunshot wound to my arm.

JACK
How did that happen?

MOLLY
My squad and I were on a rescue mission during the Fall of Saigon. I was a member of Operation Frequent Wind, and the North had its people break through the gates of the U.S. embassy, ready to attack the diplomats and the troops of the United States. It was a dangerous rescue mission that we had to cast helicopters out to sea, and carry how many we could.
(a long beat)
When the North broke through, I tried to save this kid. This poor kid who lost her parents during the Easter Offensive that I took her in and raised her as if she were my own.
(another long beat)
When she was struggling to make her way to my helicopter, I got out and tried to save her, but the North shot me in the arm, and while I survived, she didn't: The bullet went through her head, instantly killing her. Out of vengeance, I turned my helicopter on, and fired upon the North.

Feeling sorry, Jack tears up.

JACK
I'm sorry: I can't imagine what Vietnam did to you.

MOLLY
Well, at least you never experienced Vietnam through your eyes.

JACK
In a way, I kind of did.
(beat)
(MORE)

JACK (CONT'D)
When I was touring in Iraq, two years after 9/11, a friend of mine and I encountered what we thought were members of al-Qaeda in Baghdad, but it turns out to be a bunch of kids. We relayed it to our superiors, but they wanted us to open fire on the camp. My friend and I refused at first, but then, members of al-Qaeda showed up and massacred the village, leaving us no choice but to open fire on them and the rest of the villagers.
(a long beat)
When our superiors found out about it, instead of them reprimanding and sending us to the stockade, they congratulated us for following orders, never once thinking of the villagers. They were viewed as collateral damage to ensure that we win the war.
(another long beat)
When we got back, people who were opposed to the war called us murderers, and they were right. So, my friend and I vowed to never speak about it, and went our separate ways.

MOLLY
Have you spoken to your friend since then?

JACK
Sadly, no: He killed himself, easing his conscience. If only I could've reached out sooner, he would still be alive.

MOLLY
(beat)
The past is in the past, Jack: What we do now and how we go about our lives to ensure a better future, that's something worth fighting for.

JACK
Amen to that.
(noticing the clock)
Oh, jeez: I gotta go. Thanks for tonight.

MOLLY
You're welcome. Here, let me walk you to your car.

JACK
You have a nice family. If Adrienne was alive today, we would've had kids like yours.

MOLLY
Maybe you just need to find the right woman.

JACK
I tried, but no one will come close to Adrienne.

MOLLY
Can I ask you something?

JACK
Sure.

MOLLY
Your wife: What was she like?

JACK
Sweet, caring, kind-hearted, funny, dependable, and an all-around nice girl.

MOLLY
You love her, don't you? I can tell by the twinkle in your eye.

JACK
(smiling)
I do: She saw and brought out the best in me when I couldn't do it myself. Did I ever mention that she was pregnant when she was killed?

MOLLY
No.

JACK
She was: It was a son. We hoped to name him Jack, like me.
(beat)
I miss her every day. I'll see you tomorrow.

MOLLY
Before you go, can I ask you one more question?

JACK
Shoot.

MOLLY
(beat)
Today at the school, I overheard you calling yourself the Ebenezer Scrooge of Halloween. What did you mean by that?

JACK
It was Adrienne's favorite holiday. Now you know.

MOLLY
Now I know: See you tomorrow, kid.

JACK
See you tomorrow. Thank you again for inviting me.

MOLLY
You're more than welcome to stop by anytime you like.

JACK
No bullshit?

MOLLY
No bullshit.

JACK
(smiling)
Thanks. See ya.

Once Jack is in his Ford Mustang, he turns the ignition on and drives off. A content Molly looks on.

INT. MORGUE - NIGHT - LATER

The graveyard shift has begun, and JAMES DALTON has clocked in. Dalton is a handsome 26-year-old, blonde-haired man. He notices Loomis, disguised as a night guard.

DALTON
Hey, who are you? What happened to Sachs?

LOOMIS
She caught the flu. I'm just filling in till the graveyard shift relieves me.

DALTON
Well, you're looking at him.

LOOMIS
Awesome, I am relieved.

Both men chuckle.

LOOMIS (CONT'D)
Well, time to head home. Oh, since this is my unofficial first day, I forgot to punch in. Would you let the boss know I was here?

DALTON
Sure, what's your name?

LOOMIS
Clay. Freddy Clay.

Dalton turns his head and spots an unused punch-card, reading Freddy Clay written in the name section.

DALTON
Man, if you keep this up, your ass is gonna get canned for sure. But, I'll tell the boss you covered for Sachs.

LOOMIS
Thanks, brother. I owe you one. Have a good night.

DALTON
You too, Fred.

Once Loomis leaves, Dalton LISTENS to his MUSIC and plays on his phone.

INT. MOLLY'S HOUSE - KITCHEN - NIGHT - LATER

Unable to sleep, Molly heads to the fridge, and drinks a glass of ice cold milk. She then notices an envelope reading, "URGENT: FOR DETECTIVE MERCER ONLY." Molly opens the envelope, and a datebook and a flash drive falls out.

At the nearest computer, Molly logs in and puts the flash drive in the port.

The flash drive reveals two folders: School Work and Amy-Whitney Work. Intrigued with the latter folder, Molly clicks on the Amy-Whitney Work folder.

Inside are a bunch of recorded videos of Amy and Whitney bullying their peers, like duct-taping a woman to a chair and throwing her off the balcony to the bouncy house. Unnerved with what she's seeing, Molly logs out of the video and unplugs the flash drive from the port.

INT. MOLLY'S HOUSE - KITCHEN - DAY

Sleeping in front of her computer, not being in use, Molly smells a cup of coffee coming her way. She wakes up and sees Jack, handing her a cup of coffee.

JACK
Good morning.

MOLLY
Morning. What time is it?

JACK
Daytime. Listen, I've been thinking about what happened at the Myers residence the other day.

MOLLY
What do you mean?

JACK
I mean: Whitney and her boyfriend were killed the night before the Myers were, but what's the connection? Think about it: If we were dealing with a serial killer who butchers people at random, it's an open-and-closed case, but these murders aren't just random.

MOLLY
Keep talking?

JACK
What if someone was targeting them because of what the Olsons and the Myers' daughters were into?
(beat)
Of course, this is just one theory I could come up with.

MOLLY
You're not that far off, Jack.

Searching for the flash drive, Molly showcases it to Jack.

JACK
Okay, it's a flash drive: So what?

MOLLY
I have to show you at the office: This is not a place suitable for this kind of flash drive.

INT. POLICE STATION - MOLLY'S OFFICE - DAY - LATER

Inside Molly's office, Jack, like Molly last night, is uncomfortable with what he sees, and turns Molly's computer monitor off.

JACK
Wow: I was right. I mean, it kind of made sense.

MOLLY
How so?

JACK
Someone related to the bullied must've heard about what Amy and Whitney did to them, and reported to the school. When the school system failed to intervene, they took matters into their own hands, and acted upon their relatives' behalf through violent means to ensure that justice is served, whether through a professional contract killer or themselves.

MOLLY
That makes sense.

JACK
Yeah, it does.

A long beat.

JACK (CONT'D)
What?

MOLLY
This case is almost too easy to be solved.

JACK
How so?

MOLLY
I mean: If someone hired a professional to assassinate their targets, they make it look like either an accident or suicide. But what we saw these past couple of days, these were brutal murders. At the hands of a psychopath no less.

JACK
What's your point?

MOLLY
I think someone wanted these murders to be directed to what's on this flash drive, thus diverting the attention away from the real perpetrators. We need to go back to the morgue, and take a look at the body.

JACK
Let's go.

The partners exit the office.

INT. MORGUE - DAY - LATER

Making their way inside the morgue, Jack and Molly spot a sleepy Dalton.

JACK
(to Dalton)
Wake up, kid.

DALTON
(startled)
Can I help you folks?

MOLLY
Yes: My name is Molly Mercer, and this is Jack Colt. We're with the LAPD, and we're here to look at the body that came here last night.

DALTON
What body?

MOLLY
The body of the Myers family murderer.

DALTON
Oh, sorry: I'm the graveyard shift guy. I'm surprised Freddy never mentioned that.

JACK
Freddy?

DALTON
Yeah: Freddy Clay. He's a newbie.

JACK
What happened to Sachs?

DALTON
Sachs had the flu, so she called Freddy to take over.

JACK
(glancing elsewhere)
That's funny.

MOLLY
What?

JACK
It seems Sachs never punched out to go home last night.

DALTON
Maybe she forgot.

JACK
(sniffing)
What's that smell?

MOLLY
(pointing)
In there.

JACK
(to Dalton)
Call for backup.

Back to his desk, Dalton dials his superiors.

DALTON
(to himself)
I am so fired.

Approaching the hall of doors, Molly and Jack open each door, and they find nothing, except the attacker's corpse, with the gapping hole dead center on his forehead.

JACK
Is it just me, or did the bullet wound get bigger?

MOLLY
Whoever was in here, they got what they were after, but that doesn't explain the smell.

JACK
True: It definitely smells like rotting corpse.

The partners discover the source of the foul scent: the bathroom. Armed to a T, Molly and Jack enter the bathroom, and find the stalls clear, but the shower room, that's a different story.

Removing the shower curtain, Molly and Jack are in shock at what they find: the Night Guard's mutilated corpse, hung like Jesus on a cross.

DALTON
(puking)
Fuck me.

JACK
(to Dalton)
Get a medic down here: NOW!

INT. MORGUE - DAY - LATER

Investigating the murder of the night guard, the CSI team and forensics observe the crime scene. Holding a photographic copy of Loomis's shoeprint in hand, Jack presents it to Molly.

JACK
Look at this.

MOLLY
(observing the photo)
It's a boot: People wear boots part of the time, especially serial killers.

JACK
Yes, but this type of boot is military based. I haven't seen this type of footwear since Iraq.

MOLLY
Why don't we ask the night watchman, and get his opinion?

Molly and Jack approach a terrified Dalton.

MOLLY (CONT'D)
Hey, kid: How are you holding up?

DALTON
I'm fucked, aren't I?

MOLLY
No, no, no: I promise you're not going to lose your job. We need to ask you a few questions about this guy...

DALTON
Clay. Freddy Clay.

MOLLY
Freddy.

JACK
(chuckling)
Oh, that's cute.

MOLLY
(to Jack)
Shut up, man.

JACK
Yeah: Let's put an ABP out on Freddy Krueger.

MOLLY
Shut up.
(to Dalton)
Now, what can you tell us about him? Like height: What's his height? Is he like my height or my partner's?

DALTON
(pointing to Jack)
His.

MOLLY
Okay, great: That's a good start. What about hair: Did he have hair?

DALTON
(nodding)
Black.

MOLLY
Great, great.
(to a patrolman)
Go get me a pen and paper. Now.
(to Dalton)
Okay, kid: One more question. Was there anything that stuck you in your interaction with Freddy? Like a tattoo, scar, or something.

DALTON
Well, he had a chain.

MOLLY
Chain?

JACK
Chain?

MOLLY
Chain. Chain, like a necklace. What kind of necklace was it? Was it a Kay Jewelers necklace for men?

Shaking his head, Dalton points to Jack's dogtags. A beat.

DALTON
It was that.

Suddenly, this revelation stuns both Molly and Jack.

MOLLY
That?

DALTON
Yeah, silver with words branded on the front.

JACK
Are you sure?

A confident Dalton nods. Satisfied with their questioning, Molly and Jack leave Dalton with the authorities, obviously for his protection as a material witness.

JACK (CONT'D)
Molly, these are military approved dogtags. Anyone who enlists gets these.

MOLLY
Military footwear and dogtags: What the hell have we gotten into here?

JACK
Exactly.
(observing a remorseful Dalton)
Looks like the kid will need a shit ton of therapy. He's never gonna recover from this.

INT. THE MYERS RESIDENCE - DAY - LATER

Returning to the Myers residence, Molly and Jack search for clues they might have overlooked.

JACK
What the hell are we doing here?

MOLLY
Looking for a connection.

JACK
Connection for what?

MOLLY
We were wrong about the previous connection.

JACK
The bullying connection?

MOLLY
Exactly: The people responsible wanted us to think the bullying videos had Whitney and the Myers family killed to ensure that justice for the bullied was served.

JACK
But you think otherwise?

MOLLY
Exactly.
(finding the evidence)
I'll be damned.

JACK
What?

MOLLY
Look at this.

Turning around, Molly showcases a photo of Amy's dad and Calvin, along with other people surrounding the two men. There is a sign reading, "L.A. COUNTY VETERANS ADMINISTRATION BOARD."

MOLLY (CONT'D)
That's the connection.

INT. VA CLINIC - DAY

It is Whitney's memorial service today. Family and friends gather to mourn the loss of their loved one. Jack, still in his street clothes, observes and pays his respects.

Not too far from the service, and on the other side of the clinic, Molly and Calvin converse, but silence fills the room.

MOLLY
Are you going to tell me about it, Calvin?

CALVIN
Tell you about what?

MOLLY
Don't bullshit me. Whitney was murdered for nothing. She was murdered to put you in your place. To make sure you don't rattle the cage.

CALVIN
(chuckling)
Rattle who's cage?

MOLLY
Easy.

Removing a can of Ice Breakers from his coat pocket, Calvin is startled.

CALVIN
Relax, Molly.

MOLLY
Fuck that.
(long beat)
When you called me the day before Whitney died, what was the call really about?

CALVIN
I told you, Molly: I haven't seen you in two decades, and I wanted to catch up--

MOLLY
Don't blow this shit off, Calvin: You, and Amy's father, were going to fink.

CALVIN
Fink? Molly, I have no idea what the hell you're talking about.

MOLLY
I think you do. You were going to blow the whistle, so they killed your daughter. They hired someone to brutally murder your little girl, answer me.

CALVIN
For fuck's sakes, Molly: I have a family.

MOLLY
We'll put you and your family in police protection.

CALVIN
You can't protect us. You don't know them like I do.

MOLLY
Introduce me to them. I got all day.

CALVIN
(sighing)
It goes back to the early days of the CIA. My father was one of the original project managers of the MK-Ultra program. The plan was to have average, ordinary American citizens volunteer to serve their country through artificial means. What they were really doing was conditioning them to be assassins for the United States government.

MOLLY
What kinds of conditioning?

CALVIN

LSD and torture: physical and psychological. The program was a success as a result. They were able to keep the Cold War from reaching the brink of World War III. There were a couple of hiccups, however.

MOLLY

Hiccups?

CALVIN

One of them was Lee Harvey Oswald. He volunteered to be in the program, and they had him tested to see how he would react if he saw someone going to assassinate the President. Unfortunately, under the influence of the conditioning he endured, Oswald thought he was still taking the test over again, but in a real world setting. So, to prevent him from blabbing about the program, the CIA and the project managers hired Jack Ruby to silence Oswald as compensation for his mob connections as their money helped keep the program fully funded. The second hiccup, however, was when Ted Kaczynski made his face known around the world as the Unabomber, the Feds got to him before the CIA did.

(pause)

So, instead of silencing Kaczynski like they did with Oswald, the CIA had my father and his partners put the program on ice and erase all the evidence connected to them and their test subjects.

A long beat.

CALVIN (CONT'D)

After I joined the agency, years later, we brought the program back from its dormancy.

MOLLY

Go on.

CALVIN

In response to 9/11, the CIA wanted to revitalize the program, but they wanted to iron out the bugs, so they hired a group called Dark Horse, comprised of ex-military personnel and scientists. We used the same conditioning as before, but Dark Horse added a visual component to the proceedings.

MOLLY

What visual component?

CALVIN

Horror films. We had our test subjects believe they were Michael Myers, Freddy Krueger, Jason Voorhees, and they were killing all the characters from their respective film franchises when in actuality, they were toppling dictatorships and terrorist regimes.

(pause)

And to put icing on the cake: our current test subjects are former military veterans, traumatized by the wars in Iraq and Afghanistan. The kicker is: They were led to believe the program would help them readjust to civilian life. Ironic, isn't it?

MOLLY

You son-of-a-bitch! If you were getting ready to back out, why did they kill Whitney, but not you?

CALVIN

They need me, Molly.

MOLLY

Why?

CALVIN

My clinic: It's the perfect front. That way one of the patients volunteer, we can write it off as an escapee, and it'll be the police's job to classify the subjects as missing persons, diverting attention away from my involvement.

MOLLY
Unbelievable.

CALVIN
This is just business, Molly.

Rage consumes Molly.

MOLLY
Not anymore: This is personal.

CALVIN
Molly, these men are trained professionals.

MOLLY
I want to know about the next testing date. I want to know about when you're going live with the program.

CALVIN
Molly, I have said too much. These men are going to kill me. Goddamnit Molly, I am in this too deep.

Out of nowhere, a masked assassin, dressed like horror movie villain, bursts through the door, attacks Molly and brutally stabs Calvin to death. Too late, Molly opens fire on the masked killer, alerting the attention of the parishioners and Jack, who is in hot pursuit of the killer.

Back at the office, Molly approaches her ex-husband, now dead ex-husband.

MOLLY
I guess they didn't need you after all, you son-of-a-bitch.

On foot, Jack jumps on the killer, and the latter's mask pops off. The killer is revealed to be Loomis, and he and Jack exchange eye contact. As Loomis hops up, Jack opens fire, but the bullets miss Loomis. Then, Molly joins her partner.

MOLLY (CONT'D)
Did you get him?

JACK
Not yet.

I/E. VAN

Driving up to the clinic, Loomis's men open the door, and their boss jumps in. The van then drives off. The VAN DRIVER hands Loomis the phone.

DRIVER
Sir, it's Lancaster.

LOOMIS
(snatching the phone)
Yes, sir?

LANCASTER (O.S.)
Is it done?

LOOMIS
Yes, sir: Mister Olson has been silenced, but we have a bigger problem.

INT. ABANDONED HIGH SCHOOL

While on the phone, Lancaster's scientists prep the subjects for deployment.

LANCASTER
What seems to be the problem?

LOOMIS (O.S)
Mister Olson spoke the police, sir.

LANCASTER
Did you kill them?

LOOMIS
No, sir: I didn't have time.

LANCASTER
So, they might know our entire operation?

INT. VAN

Disappointment fills Loomis's face.

LOOMIS
That is correct, sir.

LANCASTER (O.S.)
That is very disappointing, Loomis:
I think we need to exterminate the
problem before going to Washington.
Come back to base.

LOOMIS
Yes, sir.

Loomis hangs up.

ENT. DOWNTOWN - NIGHT

Patrolling the Los Angeles nightlife, Jack approaches his contact, a former Special Forces sniper turn NSA operative by the name of PAULINE. She is slightly older than Jack. Not too far away, Molly observes.

JACK
Pauline, long time.

PAULINE
It certainly has been awhile.

JACK
You got what I asked?

PAULINE
First off: This incident never
happened, and we never spoke.

JACK
Understood?

PAULINE
So, here is the information on Dark
Horse.

Showing a file on Dark Horse, Pauline flips through war photos, redacted statements, and a dossier on each member of Dark Horse, but something twinkles in Jack's eyes.

JACK
Wait, go back.

Pauline flips back a couple of pages of the dossier, and Jack spots the information pertaining to Lancaster and Loomis.

PAULINE
Do you recognize the names?

JACK
Only one.
(beat)
Thank you, Pauline. I owe you one.

Satisfied, Pauline hands the files to Jack.

PAULINE
I hope this has been helpful.

JACK
It has. Thank you.

Once they say their goodbyes, Pauline disappears into the nightlife. Jack turns to Molly, showing the files on Dark Horse. Suddenly, out of nowhere, Loomis and his cohorts drive up and puts two bullets in Jack's chest, flying him to the ground.

Once that's done, Loomis and his men drive off. Then, Molly rushes over and treats Jack's wounds. Then, Molly finds a bulletproof vest underneath Jack's shirt. Tapping on the vest, Jack awakens.

JACK (CONT'D)
Oh, God: That hurts. That fucking hurts. Now, I'm pissed. I'm so pissed.

MOLLY
Thank God you were wearing your vest: I don't need another partner. Do you want me to take you to the hospital?

JACK
Yeah sure.
(a long beat)
Wait, wait.

MOLLY
What?

JACK
The guy who shot me. The guy who shot me.

Snagging the file, Jack shows Molly the dossier on Loomis.

JACK (CONT'D)
That's the same sneaky son-of-a-bitch that slashed Olson.

MOLLY
Are you sure?

JACK
I never forget a cocksucker.

Removing the vest, Jack feels the residual pain from the gunshot's blast.

MOLLY
So, what now?

JACK
We have the documents, and we have the identities of the people responsible, I think this calls for a weekend in Vegas.

MOLLY
I'm serious, Jack. We need to put the word out so we can have them face the justice system.

JACK
No, no, no: They would be long gone once they find out the heat is on their trail.
(beat)
I have an idea.

MOLLY
What?

JACK
Why don't we call up every news station, and tell them I was killed in an officer involved shooting, that way they think they were successful.

MOLLY
Why?

JACK
Because, if they don't know that I survived their assassination attempt, they would go about their business.

MOLLY
(smiling)
But they won't know what hit them when we find them. Brilliant. That's brilliant.

In the midst of the partners' jubilation, a RADIO DISPATCHER dispatches them.

DISPATCHER (O.S.)
Detectives Colt and Mercer, do you have a copy? Detectives Colt and Mercer, do you have a copy?

MOLLY
Copy, dispatch: Go ahead.

DISPATCHER (O.S.)
We received a call regarding a dead body found near your neighborhood.

MOLLY
Can you get Stan and Steve on that? I'm kind of busy.

DISPATCHER (O.S.)
The dead body had your name and dating profile number.

MOLLY
Yeah, and I bet he looks like one of those Wall Street brokers.

DISPATCHER (O.S.)
How did you know that, Detective?

Realizing the situation, Molly rushes to the drivers' seat.

MOLLY
Get in the car. Get in the car now!

JACK
What's wrong?

MOLLY
I had a date tonight.

With the ignition on and the SIRENS BLARING on the ROOF, Molly drives like a bat out of hell, and heads to her house.

I/E. MOLLY'S HOUSE - NIGHT - LATER

Parking on the grass, Molly and Jack exit the vehicle. They notice the door broken into. Whipping out their pistols, they tiptoe inside the house, searching for either Loomis and his cohorts, or Molly's kids.

Suddenly, a THUMP from behind the WALL is heard. Approaching the source, and arming themselves, Molly and Jack stand by the door. Counting to three, using their fingers, Molly opens the door and sees Natalie and Max, crying their eyes out.

MOLLY
Oh my God: Natalie, Max. Come here, come here. Are you both alright?

Putting her gun away, Molly tightly embraces her two youngest children.

MOLLY (CONT'D)
Where's Olivia?

NATALIE
They took her, Mommy.

MOLLY
Who? Who took her?

MAX
The boogeymen. The boogeymen has her, and they're going to kill her.

MOLLY
Not if I have anything to say about.
(beat)
You both are safe, and that's all that matters right now, but I promise: I will get Olivia back. You can count on that.

Molly hugs her children again. Then, the PHONE RINGS.

MOLLY (CONT'D)
(picking up the phone)
Mercer?

LOOMIS (O.S.)
You have a very beautiful daughter, Detective Mercer. It'll be a shame if anything were to happen to her.

MOLLY
Let me speak to her.

LOOMIS (O.S.)
You'll see her soon enough. Stand by the phone: We'll be in touch.

On the other end of the line, Loomis hangs up.

MOLLY
(to Jack)
They have Olivia. The bastards took my little girl.

With Molly leading Max and Natalie upstairs, Jack stays. Furious anger consumes Molly's new partner.

INT. POLICE STATION - NIGHT - LATER

Scrambling for a search party, the entire LAPD are in disarray. Meanwhile in the captain's office, her PHONE RINGS.

GRANT
Captain Grant?

LOOMIS (O.S.)
Yeah, this is Jason McClane of KTLA, and we understand that there was an officer involved shooting.

Spotting Lynn, Grant snaps her fingers and Lynn enters her office. Lynn then overhears the conversation.

GRANT
That's right: Detective Jack Colt was shot and killed tonight. His body is being transported to the county morgue. What did you say your name was?

LOOMIS (O.S.)
Thank you, Captain. That's all the information we needed.

On the other end of the phone, Loomis hangs up.

GRANT
(to Lynn)
Call phone records and have them pull up the number that called me: I think we got the son-of-a-bitch.

INT. ABANDONED HIGH SCHOOL

With a shit-eating grin on his face, Loomis spots Lancaster.

LOOMIS
Colt is out of the picture.

LANCASTER
Good. We need to take Mercer alive, and see what she knows.

LOOMIS
What makes you think she'll talk?

LANCASTER
We have her daughter: A parent will go through great lengths to save their children.

Both Lancaster and Loomis observe a bound and gagged Olivia.

LANCASTER (CONT'D)
Too bad: She would've been useful to us.

LOOMIS
How so?

LANCASTER
Under our control, she would use her beauty to bait and slay global leaders.

Scared for her life, Olivia fears a sinisterly smiling Lancaster.

INT. MOLLY'S HOUSE - KITCHEN - NIGHT - LATER

With the police escorting Natalie and Max out of the house to an undisclosed location, Molly and Jack observe the Halloween decorations.

JACK
They are going to kill you and her regardless. You know that, right?

MOLLY
Yeah.

JACK
If you want to save your daughter, we have to do this my way. Show no mercy and never let your guard down.

MOLLY
That's not going to happen. Not on my watch.

JACK
This is going to get bloody from here on out, Molly: Are you sure you're up for it?

MOLLY
(facing Jack)
Are you really that insane, or are the stories I hear about you true?

JACK
You're going to have to trust me.

The PHONE RINGS.

JACK (CONT'D)
It's them.

MOLLY
(answering the phone)
Mercer?

LANCASTER (O.S.)
We don't want the girl: We want to know the information Olson told you before he died. If you cooperate, we'll let her go, but you have to come with us. Understood?

MOLLY
Yeah, I do.

LANCASTER (O.S)
Good: Lake Dolores Waterpark. 9:00am sharp. No police. If you're late or don't show up, or if the police follow you, the girl dies.

Lancaster, on the other end of the line, hangs up. Fury consumes Molly like never before.

EXT. LAKE DOLORES WATERPARK - DAY

Not too far way from the destination, Jack, armed with a sniper rifle, hops out of the Kia Soul. Once the Kia Soul drives off, Jack, with his sniper rifle and bullets, bolts to Lake Dolores Waterpark's visitor center's rooftop.

Once Molly arrives to the Lake Dolores Waterpark itself, now abandoned, she exits her vehicle. Once Jack reaches the top of the visitor center, Jack arms himself. The two partners, from two different vantage points, spot an armored truck and a snazzy Cadillac approach Molly.

Exiting the Cadillac, Loomis approaches Molly.

LOOMIS
Mercer?

MOLLY
Yeah, that's right. It seems you're a little late getting here this morning.

LOOMIS
We had a minor setback.

Snapping his fingers, one of Loomis's men snatches Olivia, badly bruised. This angers Molly.

OLIVIA
(seeing her mother)
Mom?

MOLLY
It's okay, sweetheart: Everything will be just fine.
(to Loomis)
Lay one more hand on her, the deal's off. Got that?

LOOMIS
I got it. Now, come quietly with us, and we'll let your daughter go.

MOLLY
Let her go now.

LOOMIS
Like I said: We'll let your daughter go after you come with us. But, first: Remove any weapons off of your person.

MOLLY
You got it, pal.

Reaching inside her pockets, Molly pulls out what looks like plastic explosives attached to a detonator.

MOLLY (CONT'D)
It's active.

On the rooftop, observing the commotion, Jack doesn't have a clear shot.

JACK
(whispering to himself)
Goddamnit Molly, get out of the way. Get out of the way.

Back on the ground, Loomis' men are dumbfounded.

LOOMIS
You're bluffing. You're an officer of the law: You wouldn't risk your own daughter's safety.

MOLLY
Guess what, asshole: I'm not a cop today.

LOOMIS
(reasoning with Molly)
Detective Mercer, don't be stupid: Look at the hardware. Look at all this manpower. You're outnumbered and outmanned. Besides, Colt is not here to save your ass.

MOLLY
I don't care. If she's gonna die, she'll die by my hands.

LOOMIS
No: I don't think so.

Reaching for his gun, Loomis grazes Molly, to which she activates the detonator to five seconds. She then throws the detonator to the ground.

LOOMIS (CONT'D)
(to his men)
Down. Everybody down.

JACK
(observing)
Come on, baby. Come on.

The detonator reaches zero, and the explosives explodes, but it is revealed to be fireworks.

LOOMIS
It's just fireworks.

JACK
(to himself)
Showtime.

With a clear shot, and high above the ground, Jack opens fire.

GOON
Where's that coming from?

LOOMIS
Damnit, it's Colt.

As Jack continues firing upon Loomis and his goons, Molly tears a piece of her plaid shirt and wraps it around her wound.

MOLLY
(to Olivia)
Olivia, run. Run.

Escaping their grasp, Olivia runs inside the building. After that, Molly reaches for her gun and opens fire, killing about a couple of goons. Back on the rooftop, Jack doesn't know that someone is approaching him from behind.

JACK
(to himself)
Okay, get it lined up.
(spotting Loomis)
Sayonara, motherfucker.

Then, the mysterious person is revealed to be Lancaster, pointing a loaded weapon at Jack.

LANCASTER
You have guts, son: I'll give you that, but this is where we have to draw a line in the sand.

Lowering his weapon, Jack gives himself up.

LANCASTER (O.S.) (CONT'D)
(on the walkie-talkie)
Come in, Loomis. Come in, Loomis.

LOOMIS
(answering)
Yes, sir?

LANCASTER (O.S.)
We got Colt.

LOOMIS
Roger that, sir.
(to his men)
We got Colt. Go get the girl.

With only Molly firing on all cylinders, the surviving goons chase after Olivia on foot while the remainder of the goons fire warning shots directly at Molly. She then surrenders. Now on the ground, and is about to regroup with Loomis, Lancaster holds Colt at gunpoint.

LANCASTER
You look familiar, Colt: Have we met?

JACK
Yeah: You're Alan Lancaster, leader of Dark Horse, and my former drill instructor during basic training.

LANCASTER
I knew you looked familiar. As I recall, you were one of the best marksmen in the class.

JACK
Yep. Too bad you'll be biting the bullet soon.

LANCASTER
We'll see about that, son.

Finally catching up to Olivia, Loomis's goons drag her back to Loomis, which then turns around. With Dark Horse gaining control of the situation, Molly and Jack have failed.

INT. ABANDONED HIGH SCHOOL - NIGHT

With Molly and Jack separated, Jack is in a darkly lit men's room. Tied to handlebars inside the shower room portion of the men's room, and via water from the shower head, Jack awakens. Loomis approaches Jack.

LOOMIS
Rise and shine, sleepy head.
(a long beat)
Still tired. Too bad. I want you to see what we got planned for you.

Jack notices OLAF, a very tattooed man.

JACK
Who's the tat?

LOOMIS
Olaf, this is Jack Colt. Best marksman in the military.
(MORE)

LOOMIS (CONT'D)
Jack, this is Olaf. Best torturer in all of Sweden.

JACK
Good to know.

LOOMIS
You have to understand, Jack, that our problem, however big or small, is your problem too.

JACK
Oh yeah: What kind of problem do I have?

LOOMIS
You see, we have Mercer, and my superior officer considers you unimportant, but I beg to differ.

JACK
Go on: I'm listening.

LOOMIS
Now, our problem is that we are supposed to be in Washington right now, showcasing our volunteers how well they do in combat.

JACK
Uh-huh: Using horror films as a visual component for the MK-Ultra program.
(a long beat)
What are you surprised? Molly told me what Olson told her about what you guys do to our brothers- and sisters-in-arms. Torturing them, drugging them, and brainwashing them to think like they're slasher film villains.

LOOMIS
Yeah, well: You don't know the whole story, Jack. The United States government commissioned the MK-Ultra program to be revived to search and destroy terrorist regimes--

JACK
And topple dictatorships around the globe.
(MORE)

JACK (CONT'D)
Again, that's what Olson told Molly before you silenced him, and that's what she told me. So, why don't you shut the fuck up and kill me already?

LOOMIS
It's not that simple, Jack: We want to know what else Olson said because if we don't find out, there will be dozens upon dozens of cops surrounding the airport.

JACK
I could see how that could be bad.

LOOMIS
Absolutely, and it would be ideal to find out what you, Mercer, and the rest of the boys in blue know. If you tell me right away, I'll make sure your death is quick and painless.

JACK
I said my piece, so you should get on with the torturing.

LOOMIS
(to Olaf)
Olaf.

Snagging a butcher knife from his belt, Olaf approaches Jack.

JACK
What's he doing?

LOOMIS
Olaf here is going to slash and dash your ass like a Thanksgiving turkey.

JACK
I guess we're in it for the long haul because I don't know shit.

Gaining Loomis' seal of approval, Olaf slashes Jack's ribcage, and the latter screams.

LOOMIS
Again.

Turning him around, Olaf knicks Jack's back, thus making the latter scream even harder.

JACK
I'll kill you. I'll fucking kill you all.

LOOMIS
Tell me what else Olson said.

Without orders, Olaf continues torturing Jack. On the other side of the school, Molly is also being tortured, and while it is not as gruesome as Jack's, it is still bloody.

LANCASTER
The information, Detective Mercer.

MOLLY
Go fuck yourself.

LANCASTER
(beat)
What was that? I couldn't hear: Would you repeat that?

MOLLY
Why don't you get some fucking hearing aids? I told you to go fuck yourself.

LANCASTER
I'll be more lenient with you since you and I never officially met, even if we served in the same war, I have zero tolerance for those who swear.

Snatching a bottle of alcohol, Lancaster removes Molly's makeshift bandage and pours the alcohol on her wound, making her scream.

MOLLY
I hope you burn in hell. I hope you burn in hell.

LANCASTER
This is getting us nowhere.
(to one of his men)
Go get her daughter.

Once the henchman leaves, Molly's torture ceases. As that happens, a bloodied and scarred Jack screams at the top of his lungs, but he has found his light at the end of the tunnel: an open gap in the knots.

Pretending to be passed out, Olaf stops torturing Jack.

OLAF

Well, that was easier than I thought.

LOOMIS

Check him.

OLAF

(checking Jack's pulse)

He's still breathing, but it looks like he'll need medical attention.

LOOMIS

Cut him loose. Patch him up. We'll try this again later.

After Loomis leaves the men's room, Olaf disarms himself and unties and patches up Jack. Once that's done, Jack wakes up and attacks Olaf, during which, Jack snaps Olaf's neck. Grabbing his weapons and Olaf's Members Only jacket, Jack exits the men's room.

Back at the gymnasium, Olivia is presented to Molly. Mother and daughter embrace.

MOLLY

Are you okay, sweetie?

OLIVIA

I'm fine.

Then, Loomis shows up.

LANCASTER

Did Colt talk?

LOOMIS

No, Olaf did so much damage to his body, he's back there patching him up.

LANCASTER

Why aren't you back there looking after Olaf?

LOOMIS

Colt is passed out, sir. I trust Olaf: He's never let us down before.

LANCASTER

Okay, I trust you, Loomis.

LOOMIS
(observing Molly)
What about Mercer? Did she talk?

LANCASTER
Nope, but I think we have an ace in the hole.
(pointing to Olivia)
Make her feel special. I want Mercer to watch.

Dragging Olivia to a chair, Loomis removes her blouse, exposing her chest to Loomis' visible eye.

MOLLY
If you two do anything to my daughter, you both are going to pay.

LANCASTER
Save it, Mercer: This ain't the movies. The bad guys always win.

Bursting through the door, Jack opens fire on Lancaster and his goons.

LANCASTER (CONT'D)
Kill that asshole.

Lancaster's goons retaliate, but Jack tags a few henchmen with his bullets.

JACK
Loomis. Lancaster.

With the colonel and his right-hand man running away, it's only Jack, Molly, and Olivia.

MOLLY
Members Only jacket, huh?

JACK
Yeah, and it surprisingly fits me well.

Rushing to Molly's aid, Jack unties her and then Olivia.

JACK (CONT'D)
Are you both okay?

MOLLY
Little wounded, but I'm fine.

OLIVIA
I'm okay too.

JACK
Let's get the heck out of here!

Suddenly, out of nowhere, a brainwashed test subject attacks Jack, who then engages in knife-to-knife combat. While the brainwashed test subject overpowers Jack, the latter gains the upper hand, and stabs the brainwashed test subject in the forehead, effectively killing him.

JACK (CONT'D)
(to the girls)
Let's go.

EXT. ABANDONED HIGH SCHOOL

Outside the abandoned high school is the Halloween dance, where the students and teachers dress up like famous movie or television characters. Bursting out the door, Jack spots one of Lancaster's goons and shoots him in the head.

Coasting through the crowd undetected, Loomis spots Jack and the girls. Jack then responds by opening fire, causing the dance attendees to scatter and go crazy. In the midst of the stampeding craziness, Jack fires upon Loomis.

JACK
Loomis.

Jack and Loomis trade bullets, but the latter makes his way toward the parking lot.

LOOMIS
(to the stampeding crowd)
Move you ass. Move your fucking asses.

A blue Chevy Impala crashes into Loomis.

LOOMIS (CONT'D)
(to the driver)
Hey, hey: Get out of the fucking car. Get out of the fucking car.

Violently pulling the door open, Loomis grabs the driver's costume and throws him to the ground. Once that's done, Loomis enters the vehicle, rolls down the window and then spots Jack and they again trade bullets in front of a frightened crowd. Afterwards, Loomis drives off.

As Jack rushes in Loomis' direction, a COP approaches Molly.

COP
Drop it, lady.

Proving she's a cop, Molly whips her badge out, and she succeeds.

MOLLY
It's okay: I'm a cop. Get my daughter and these people out of the line of fire, and call for backup. Tell them, "Molly Mercer needs backup at Vermont Square." Do it.

COP
Yes, ma'am.

EXT. DOWNTOWN

With the cop protecting Olivia and the dance attendees, Molly joins Jack. He is hurling bullets at Loomis, speeding down the road. Now that Loomis is out of his sight, Jack barrels through the street, with Molly struggling to keep up.

As Jack is a faster runner than her, Molly rests.

MOLLY
JACK! JACK!

JACK
(stopping)
Yeah.

MOLLY
The on-ramp. He's heading to the on-ramp.

JACK
You gonna make it?

MOLLY
I'll be fine. Just cut through Broadway and Gage, you'll beat him to the on-ramp. Quickly now, go.

Thanks to Molly's directions, Jack rushes to the on-ramp before his and Molly's nemesis does. As that happens, Molly checks and loads her gun.

MOLLY (CONT'D)
Colonel Lancaster, your turn to do the dying.

Gathering her second wind, a vengeful Molly searches for Lancaster. During that time, Loomis searches for the on-ramp. In the nick of time, Jack chases Loomis' tail.

SERIES OF SHOTS: JACK AND LOOMIS'S ROAD RAGE

-Noticing Jack in his rearview mirror, Loomis drives faster and opens fire. By doing that, he struggles with the steering wheel.

-Still on foot, Jack presses the trigger. Once he's out of bullets, Jack reloads.

-Reaching the on-ramp to freedom, Loomis maniacally laughs, but his euphotic state ceases when a pickup truck crashes into Loomis.

-Witnessing the crash, Jack books it.

-The pickup truck's DRIVER exits his vehicle. He is an overweight, middle-aged man with a baseball cap as headwear.

DRIVER
(checking on Loomis)
Hey buddy, are you okay?

LOOMIS
(glaring)
You tried to kill me, you son-of-a-bitch.

-Using his strength, Loomis punches through the driver's stomach, crawling his hand up inside the latter's body, and rips out his heart, effectively killing the driver.

-After that, Loomis spots Jack approaching, the former exits the stolen Impala and runs to an unknown destination. With both protagonist and antagonist on foot, they continue trading bullets.

-With neither of the men feeling an inch of tiredness, Loomis gains further distance between him and Jack. This comes to his advantage when he spots an SUV.

-Pointing at the SUV and its inhabitants, Loomis slings the door open.

LOOMIS (CONT'D)
Out. Out now.

-The SUV's inhabitants evacuate their vehicle, and Loomis takes control.

Then, Loomis and Jack play a very fucked-up version of chicken, with Loomis violently pressing the pedal and Jack running toward the stolen SUV.

-In the nick of time, Jack jumps out of the way, and Loomis has a clean getaway. The SUV's inhabitants help a furious Jack.

JACK
Get back.

Failed in his pursuit of Loomis, Jack regroups with Molly.

END OF SERIES

INT. ABANDONED HIGH SCHOOL

Pressing a needle into the volunteer's heads, and pouring gasoline over the bodies, Lancaster and one of his GOONS eradicate all the evidence regarding the revived MK-Ultra program.

LANCASTER
They all dead?

GOON
Every volunteer's life functions
and programming have ceased.

LANCASTER
Burn it.

Lighting a match, the Goon slings it and a fire erupts, engulfing the dead volunteers' bodies in flames.

LANCASTER (CONT'D)
Grab the research, and let's get
the hell out of here.

With the research in hand, Lancaster heads to a Volkswagen beetle.

I/E. BEETLE

Making their escape, they see Molly, with vengeance in her eyes, standing in the middle of the road.

LANCASTER
(annoyed)
Kill the bitch!

The goon presses the pedal, charging toward Molly.

MOLLY
(to herself)
For my daughter, you son-of-a-bitch.

Whipping her gun out, Molly blasts bullets through the window all the way to the goon's forehead, causing the Beetle to swerve. Lancaster struggles for control over the wheel. He is successful, but Lancaster is too late to notice a truck on his left.

LANCASTER
Shit.

The truck sends the Beetle flying into the air, with the file on the revived MK-Ultra program flying out the Beetle. The file lands on the paved road while the Beetle crashes and faces east.

As Molly picks up the file, she notices the unconscious truck driver's lit cigarette drop on the gasoline, igniting a trail of flames heading in Lancaster's direction.

LANCASTER (CONT'D)
(pleading)
Please. Please. You wouldn't let a fellow military officer die, would you?

MOLLY
You betrayed your oath to protect this country. You tortured your fellow squadron, and worst of all: You fucked up my daughter.
(beat)
Happy trails, Colonel.

Screaming for his life, the flame reaches the Beetle, exploding upon impact, with Lancaster and his dead goon roasting inside. Satisfied, and with evidence in tow, Molly leaves.

EXT. HIGH SCHOOL

Spotting Jack, Molly embraces him.

JACK
You okay?

MOLLY
I am now.

JACK
Where's Lancaster?

MOLLY
Let's just say he's cooking up a storm on the back side of the school.

Both partners chuckle.

MOLLY (CONT'D)
What about Loomis? Did you catch the son-of-a-bitch?

JACK
No, he got away. Probably halfway to Mexico by now.

MOLLY
Which way was he going?

JACK
West.

MOLLY
But, Mexico is south.

JACK
You're right: I didn't think about that.
(beat)
Holy shit: I know where he's going.

MOLLY
Where?

JACK
Get in the car: I'll tell you.

MOLLY
I'm driving. I'm a lot faster on the wheel.

With Molly and Jack in the front side of a squad car, the car speeds off.

I/E. SQUAD CAR

Pressing the pedal down, Jack heads in Loomis's direction.

MOLLY
If he's not going to Mexico, then where is he going?

JACK
He's heading to the airport.

MOLLY
Why?

JACK
In case shit went south, Loomis would regroup with Lancaster and flee the country.

MOLLY
They aren't.

JACK
But Loomis doesn't know that.

MOLLY
Are you sure, Jack? Are you one hundred percent sure he'll be at your house?

JACK
Trust me.

Activating the police sirens, Molly speeds along the highway.

EXT. AIRPORT - NIGHT - LATER

Arriving at the airport, Loomis drives up to the gate, where there's a brightly lit guard shack in the center. Inside the shack are two GUARDS, drinking coffee.

LOOMIS
(to the officers)
Excuse me: I'm a little lost, and my GPS is acting goofy. Is this Brentwood?

GUARD #1
No, this is Woodland Hills. Brentwood is seventeen miles south of here.

GUARD #2
If you want, we can help you get directions to get where you need to go.

LOOMIS
Sure, that would be much obliged.

DISPATCHER (O.S.)
Attention all units. Attention all units. Be on the lookout for possible suspect driving a blue SUV. I repeat: Be on the lookout for a possible suspect driving a blue SUV. He is armed and extremely dangerous.

Realizing who Loomis really is, the two guards snag their guns, but in cold blood, Loomis slays them and drives off. Parking the stolen car near the hangar, Loomis turns the ignition off and exits the vehicle.

Noticing that his men are murdered, Loomis arms himself and approaches the hangar.

I/E. AIRPORT HANGAR

Kicking down the door, Loomis blasts through the walls. He then searches the entire hangar, only to find it completely empty. However, Loomis spots a note. It reads: "Happy Halloween, assholes! Signed, LAPD Dicks."

Angered, Loomis finds the television on. The television airs AMC Fearfest. I Know What You Did Last Summer is a part of the lineup. Suddenly, Jennifer Love Hewitt's character's SCREAM REVERBERATES from the TELEVISION. Angry, Loomis whacks the television.

LOOMIS
(beat)
Sarah Michelle Gellar's a better final girl than you.

Continuing his search, Loomis finds no one. Suddenly, outside the hangar, Loomis's stolen SUV explodes. He then bolts outside and observes the damage. Then, Jack and Molly approach and disarm Loomis.

JACK
Damn, you're so gullible.

LOOMIS
Well played, you two. Well played.

MOLLY
Yeah, well: Your commanding officer, the colonel himself: He's barbecuing himself to an early grave. He ain't going to be much help now.

LOOMIS
You're forgetting one thing, Mercer: We still have the data to continue the program. You think you stopped us, think again. There will be one group to pick up where we left off, and continue in a new city. A new state. A new country, the list goes on and on.

MOLLY
(showcasing the file)
You mean this data: It's over, fucker.

Amused and ill-tempered, Loomis removes his jacket.

JACK
What do you say, man? You want to blow off some steam?

LOOMIS
Absolutely.

Dead center on the street, Jack and Loomis engage in mortal combat. As the duel begins, airport security and the rest of the LAPD show up.

MOLLY
(to all the officers)
Back away from the area. This is our collar. Wait until I give the word to move in.

Then, beyond the gate, the news force show up and report on Jack and Loomis's final battle.

KTLA REPORTER
What you are looking at is what appears to be a street fight between two men. One of them is a LAPD officer and the other is the suspect. No word yet on their identities.

KNBC REPORTER
My god: This is better than Pay-Per-View, folks. We are actually live in Burbank Airport, witnessing a literal street fight. I don't know about you Gale and Michael, but my money's on the Member's Only guy.

SPANISH REPORTER
(in Spanish)
Two gringos in the middle of the street fighting, and it's getting bloodier by the minute. This is no joke, everyone.

Back on the ground, a bloodied Jack removes his jacket, wraps it around Loomis's neck, and chokes him. Loomis is also bloodied. Almost about to pass out, Loomis flips Jack over and dislocates his right shoulder. This makes Jack scream.

KNBC REPORTER
Holy schnikes, y'all: The guy just broke the man's shoulders. I think the other guy just lost. This is getting really intense down there.

Kicking Loomis's face, Jack picks himself up, and heads to a neighboring hangar. He smashes his shoulder back into place, screaming in agonizing pain. Catching his second wind, Jack notices Loomis lifting himself off the ground.

Charging toward Loomis, Jack flies himself and Loomis toward an airport security's parked car, smashing the window in the process. With so much anger and violence in his heart, Jack pounds on Loomis. Having had enough, Loomis knocks Jack back to the ground.

Jumping off the car, Loomis approaches and chokes Jack.

MOLLY
Jack, Jack: Don't give up, Jack. Don't you fucking give up on me.

JACK
I'm...not.

Flipping Loomis on his back, Jack elbows him in the chest, causing Loomis to lose his breath. Jack then chokes Loomis to death.

MOLLY
Fuck him up, Jack. Fuck him up. Rip his goddamn head off.

Realizing what he has become, and what kind of path he is on, Jack releases an unconscious Loomis.

JACK
You're done, asshole.

Leaving Loomis to the LAPD, Jack approaches Molly, who then comforts her bloodied and bruised partner.

Suddenly, in the midst of being apprehended, Loomis wakes up, rips the arresting officers' guts out, and snags a gun.

Noticing this, Molly and Jack whips out their guns, and put a couple of metallic pills in Loomis's forehead, instantly killing him. Satisfied, Molly takes Jack to the hospital.

MONTAGE: DISCOVERY OF THE REVIVED MK-ULTRA PROGRAM AND AFTERMATH

-A collection of Jack and Loomis's brutal street fight appears over a local news report.

ANCHOR
Today's top story is the resurgence of the MK-Ultra program that was uncovered by these two LAPD detectives: Molly Mercer and her partner, Jack Colt. They were investigating the grisly murders of Whitney Olson and her boyfriend Rick Cohen a few nights ago when they discovered this shocking and very bizarre information.

-Jack and Molly's case goes from local to national to worldwide.

PANELIST
The United States government brainwashed the people who protect us and this great country of ours, and they had the nerve to hide this from us.

MODERATOR
So, you're saying you don't trust the United States government?

PANELIST
Oh, I do: Just not the ones who knew about the resurgence of MK-Ultra.

-Suddenly, the story of Jack and Molly's case is told via a conspiracy theory EXPERT. She showcases a photo of them.

EXPERT
These two right here, uncovered the truth behind MK-Ultra, and how the United States government, our elected officials, blatantly kept this from us, and these people right here, stop the entire government from creating a new world order on our own soil.
(tearing up)
God bless you, Colt and Mercer: The saviors of America.

-A national NEWS ANCHOR interviews a top United States SENATOR.

NEWS ANCHOR
So, what you are telling me, Senator, is that you did not know that this group of mercenaries and military scientists were holding rehabilitating soldiers against their will? Am I correct?

SENATOR
That's correct.

NEWS ANCHOR
Even though, your name is on the list of those who funded the revived MK-Ultra program.

SENATOR
When I was told about this, Colonel Lancaster told me it was for a tank he and his men were building, not this.

NEWS ANCHOR
A tank? A tank? Really. You chose Colonel Lancaster's word over whoever else knew about this. You know you can go to prison for funding something like this, right?

SENATOR
Look, I don't want to start a debate right now, but this interview is over.

END OF MONTAGE

EXT. GRAVEYARD - DAY

It is a beautiful Halloween day. The sun brightly shines high above the sky. Standing over his wife's grave, and healing from his wounds, a visibly scarred Jack cradles a carved pumpkin, and Porsha stands tall next to her daddy.

Kneeling down, Jack places the pumpkin on top of the gravestone, but this pumpkin is no ordinary pumpkin. The carving has Adrienne's face in the front. Lighting a candle inside the pumpkin, Jack places his wedding ring inside as well.

JACK
Happy Halloween, Adrienne Leigh: I love you.

Having made peace with her death, Jack, along with Porsha, strolls away.

INT. POLICE STATION - CAPTAIN'S OFFICE - DAY - LATER

Meeting with Grant, Jack, petting Porsha, notices his boss presenting Jack's Sergeant badge.

JACK
What's this?

GRANT
A shiny new name plate: What do you think? I'm reinstating you back to Sergeant.

JACK
What about Molly?

GRANT
Don't worry about her: We found her a more suitable candidate that's more her speed. Besides, I feel like after this little experience working in homicide, I figure this will be a token of gratitude.

As happy as Jack is that he's earned his Sergeant badge back, Jack places the badge down.

JACK
As much fun as I was being a sergeant, I enjoyed being a detective again.
(MORE)

JACK (CONT'D)
Not only that, I enjoyed working with Molly these past few days: I don't see anyone being Molly's partner, but me.

GRANT
Are you sure about this, Jack? If you are, you won't be getting this chance again.

JACK
I'm sure, Captain: I am much happier now than I was before.

GRANT
I can see that. Well, I guess: Carry on, Detective.

JACK
Yes, ma'am. Molly and I will be working on our reports.

GRANT
I wouldn't worry about Molly: She has the day off.

JACK
She does?

GRANT
(beat)
Jack, it's Halloween: She always has the day off when it comes to this holiday. In fact, why don't you take some time off yourself: We got this handled.

JACK
You sure? 'Cause if you need someone to cause a little havoc while solving a case, I'm your--

GRANT
Just go, Jack. We'll see you when you get back.

Picking up Porsha, Jack opens the door.

JACK
(turning around)
Thank you, Captain.

GRANT
You're welcome.

Then, Jack leaves.

EXT. MOLLY'S HOUSE - NIGHT

RINGING the DOORBELL, Jack sees Olivia, healing from her bruises, open the door.

JACK
Hi.

OLIVIA
Hi.

JACK
How are you?

OLIVIA
I'm holding up. You?

JACK
Yeah, me too.
(a long beat)
Is your mom home?

OLIVIA
Yeah, she's in the kitchen getting everything ready for the trick-or-treaters, and getting Natalie and Max's costumes ready.

JACK
That's nice.

OLIVIA
I can tell her that--

JACK
No, no: It's fine.
(beat)
Actually, I stopped by to give her something.

Reaching inside his pocket, Jack hands Olivia his Medal of Honor.

JACK (CONT'D)
It's a belated congratulatory present: I have no further use for it anymore.

OLIVIA
But, this Medal of Honor is yours.

JACK
I know: She deserved it a lot more than I do.

A long beat.

OLIVIA
Do you want to come in and help my mom?

JACK
No, I have to get going, but you have a happy Halloween, okay?

OLIVIA
Okay. See you around.

JACK
See you.

Once Jack leaves the premises, Molly rushes out the door.

MOLLY
Jack, Jack.

JACK
Yeah.

MOLLY
If you think, after everything that we went through, you can still go around town, claiming to be the Ebenezer Scrooge of Halloween, you're missing out on all the fun.

JACK
I have some news for you.

MOLLY
Shoot.

JACK
I don't hate Halloween anymore.

MOLLY
(a long beat)
I know.

JACK
Good: Still need help getting ready?

MOLLY
The more hands on deck, the better.

With Jack in tow, Molly heads back to the house.

JACK
Hey, I hope you have those scented candles to make your house smell like Halloween.

MOLLY
Like what?

JACK
Pumpkin spice.

MOLLY
Mention that again, and I'll rip your testicles off.

JACK
You'll try: Hey, would it be okay if I bring a friend to help too?

MOLLY
Sure.

Rushing back to his car, Jack opens the door and Porsha leaps onto the ground and bolts inside Molly's house.

MOLLY (CONT'D)
My kids and neighbors are not going to be pleased about this.

JACK
I have forty on Porsha scaring off the trick-or-treaters.

Inside the house, Porsha causes all sorts of mayhem.

NATALIE
Mommy, Mommy: there's a baby polar bear destroying the house.

MAX
Don't let it get into the candy.

OLIVIA
My god, what is that thing?

While Jack is amused by the destruction at the hands of Porsha, Molly, on the other hand, controls her frustration.

MOLLY
(to herself; beat)
God help us all.

Not wanting the trick-or-treaters to see the mess Porsha makes, Molly closes the door.

FADE TO BLACK.

THE END

www.ingramcontent.com/pod-product-compliance
Lightning Source LLC
LaVergne TN
LVHW050323160826
845677LV00014B/3524